# Dear Parent:

Congratulations! Your child is taking the first steps on an exciting journey. The destination? Independent reading!

**STEP INTO READING®** will help your child get there. The program offers five steps to reading success. Each step includes fun stories and colorful art. There are also Step into Reading Sticker Books, Step into Reading Math Readers, Step into Reading Phonics Readers, Step into Reading Write-In Readers, and Step into Reading Phonics Boxed Sets—a complete literacy program with something to interest every child.

## Learning to Read, Step by Step!

**Ready to Read    Preschool–Kindergarten**
• big type and easy words • rhyme and rhythm • picture clues
For children who know the alphabet and are eager to begin reading.

**Reading with Help    Preschool–Grade 1**
• basic vocabulary • short sentences • simple stories
For children who recognize familiar words and sound out new words with help.

**Reading on Your Own    Grades 1–3**
• engaging characters • easy-to-follow plots • popular topics
For children who are ready to read on their own.

**Reading Paragraphs    Grades 2–3**
• challenging vocabulary • short paragraphs • exciting stories
For newly independent readers who read simple sentences with confidence.

**Ready for Chapters    Grades 2–4**
• chapters • longer paragraphs • full-color art
For children who want to take the plunge into chapter books but still like colorful pictures.

**STEP INTO READING®** is designed to give every child a successful reading experience. The grade levels are only guides. Children can progress through the steps at their own speed, developing confidence in their reading, no matter what their grade.

Remember, a lifetime love of reading starts with a single step!

*For Peter, Emily, and Marius Jr.—M.M.-K.*

Published in the United States by Random House Children's Books, a division of Random House, Inc., 1745 Broadway, New York, NY 10019, and in Canada by Random House of Canada Limited, Toronto.

Step into Reading, Random House, and the Random House colophon are registered trademarks of Random House, Inc.

Visit us on the Web!
www.stepintoreading.com
www.randomhouse.com/kids
www.barbie.com

Educators and librarians, for a variety of teaching tools, visit us at
www.randomhouse.com/teachers

*Library of Congress Cataloging-in-Publication Data*
Man-Kong, Mary.
I can be a pet vet / by Mary Man-Kong ; illustrated by Jiyoung An.
   p. cm. — (Step into reading. Step 1)
"Barbie."
ISBN 978-0-375-86581-7 (trade) — ISBN 978-0-375-96581-4 (lib. bdg.)
I. An, Jiyoung. II. Title.   PZ7.M31215Iag 2010   [E]—dc22 2009048168

Printed in the United States of America

10 9 8 7 6 5 4 3 2

STEP INTO READING®

STEP 1

# Barbie™ i can be...

# A Pet Vet

By Mary Man-Kong

Illustrated by Jiyoung An

Random House 🏠 New York

# Barbie takes her pet to the vet.

# A vet helps pets.

# The vet checks Lacey.

# Lacey is okay.

# The busy vet needs help.

Barbie will help

the vet.

What pets will
they help?

Big dog.

# Small kittens.

Gray cat.

# Blue bird.

# Fluffy bunny.

# Bumpy turtle.

Barbie and the vet
help all the pets.

Barbie brings Ken's dog
to the scale.

# Lacey helps.

The kittens are next.

Where did they go?

# Teresa looks up.

Barbie looks down.
They find
the kittens!

Barbie pats
Nikki's sick cat.

The vet helps
the cat.

# What pet is next?

# A pony!

The pony hurt
its leg.

# The vet checks it.

Barbie and the vet
help the pony.

Barbie can be
a pet vet, too.

# Hooray for vets!
# Hooray for pets!